Haunting Desire

Desire Series
Book Two
Roxanne Rhoads

This is a work of fiction. Similarities to real people, places, or events are entirely coincidental.

HAUNTING DESIRE

First edition. February 5, 2016.

Copyright © 2016 Roxanne Rhoads.

ISBN: 979-8201178154

Written by Roxanne Rhoads.

Haunting Desire
By Roxanne Rhoads

1

Chapter One

Michigan was so different from New Orleans. I had lived in Michigan for a while, but I had not been to Kalamazoo yet. My business partner and best friend, Carrie, booked the job for me. She was a business wiz and kept everything running smoothly- the office, the books, even designed our website. She took care of the technical stuff while I did the "ghost whispering" thing.

I was so thankful when she moved from L.A. to New Orleans with me after Christien and I got together. Then after Hurricane Katrina's ghosts would not leave me alone, we relocated to Michigan. Christien has friends and business connections in Flint. She came to Michigan with us. Christien set up his office and lab outside Flint, and I opened my office in the heart of downtown. I travel all over Michigan if the case is interesting enough. Carrie assured me this one was but she didn't give me any specifics. I tried to assess a ghost situation myself before learning of outside details. I didn't like any preconceived notions or expectations to cloud my judgment.

The drive to Kalamazoo was uneventful and the city itself unremarkable, even though it was mid-September and the autumn colors were beginning. Too bad it wasn't a week or two later, I heard that's when the color show would be in full effect. It was supposed to be quite beautiful. Having lived in warm climates all of my life I had yet to witness a full-on summer to fall color show or a Michigan winter- that I was not looking forward to.

Kalamazoo looked pretty much like every other Michigan city I'd been to so far. A mix of shiny new buildings stuck between historical buildings in various states of decay.

On the outskirts of town, the business districts had seen better days. You could tell some areas were poor. Closer to downtown the once industrial buildings were in various stages of abandonment or gentrification.

The main strip of downtown Kalamazoo bustled with restaurants, shops, hotels and other businesses.

My destination, a bed and breakfast Inn, was on the outskirts of downtown Kalamazoo, in the "college town" area. As I drove, I took note of the numerous Victorians in all states- from boarded up and falling down to lived-in but long past their original glory to fully restored and beautiful.

I thought it pretentious that the Victorian I was heading to was called a castle. Yes, Victorians can be downright gorgeous, but worthy of the title castle? I had never been to one worthy of being called a castle, and I'd been to many, many Victorians. They were almost always haunted. You can't accumulate that much history without holding onto at least one restless spirit.

Every city has buildings and locations filled ghosts. Some were just more prevalent than others.

I once called New Orleans home. It is renowned as one the most haunted cities in the United States. But the devastating aftermath of Hurricane Katrina more than quadrupled the number of lost souls floating around the city. They wouldn't leave me alone. I tried to help as many as I could, but they tormented me night and day, whether they meant to or not. Their lost cries, the pushing and prodding they inflicted on me once they realized I could sense them...I finally couldn't take it anymore and left. Packed up my business and joined Christien's friends in Michigan. Now they send ghost hunting and ghost banishing work my way constantly.

Like the place I was headed now, the owner was a friend of a friend, and she had spoken with Carrie about her unique need for my services. She owned Radcliff Castle, a Victorian built in 1895 that was being renovated and turned into a bed and breakfast. That's all I knew. I never did background research because I didn't like names or historical facts to influence my investigation until after I got a feel for the place and the spirits inhabiting it.

I spotted the sign for the castle and turned to drive up a steep hill. As the house came into view, I gasped. I suddenly understood why it was called a castle. The title was not pretentious at all. This was the grandest example of a Queen Anne Victorian I had ever seen. Made of sandstone and brick the building sported turrets and towers that gave it the unquestionable look of a castle, this was Victorian elegance at its finest.

I parked my car and stepped out. The late summer sun bathed the castle in its rays, a natural spotlight to showcase the beauty of the place. I stood there in awe, absorbing the feel of the place. History clawed at my senses, but I was seeking spirits, not the heaviness of the past.

Unease hung in the air, not an eerie vibe like most haunted places had but a weird vibe, it reminded me of nervous energy, the kind you get when you're really excited about something. It was intense, full of expectation, need. Not the feel of your average haunted house.

I walked around the building cataloging details while looking for an entrance. I finally found a path that led to a long wrap around porch. The porch was quite lovely and contained small bistro dining sets, a nice touch for guests who wished to enjoy the open air.

I entered and walked up to a desk and rang the bell. While waiting, I glanced around. To my left was a formal dining room. To my right I could see a bar and various doors and openings that probably led to a kitchen and other rooms. To the left of the desk was a staircase.

A busty blonde bustled in from one of the side rooms on my right. Her attire and demeanor were all business. She must be the owner, Barbara, who Carrie had spoken with on the phone. I introduced myself.

"LizBeth, thank you so much for coming. I've heard great things about you and your skills communicating with ghosts."

"Thank you, Barbara." I got right to the point, "So have you experienced a lot of ghostly activities here?" I glanced around the castle; it sure looked like the type of place that would have ghosts. I could feel its history reaching out to me. I have been in many Victorians over the years searching for ghosts, but none this fancy. It was not truly a castle, at least not in an old world European sense, but this is definitely what passes as a castle in the US. The over the top extravagance gave it royal appeal. Once it had been referred to as Radcliff Castle. Now Barbara simply called it the Castle Inn.

"Let me show you around a bit," She gestured for me to follow her.

As we walked around, I paid close attention to details. Sometimes the smallest thing could make a difference when it came to hauntings. Occasionally it was an object that was haunted and not the location. One never knew until immersing themselves into the haunt.

On the surface, the Castle Inn was in top shape. It appeared to have been completely restored and from what I could tell everything was original, from the elaborate trim and crown molding to the built-in buffet in the large formal dining room and the bar in the back. It was breathtakingly exquisite.

I wasn't sure what to expect from this job. I didn't have many details. Just that she wanted me to check out her new Inn for spectral activity. She probably wanted me to rid the place of the spirits that would scare away customers.

Before I could ask her not to give me too many details, she was already spilling information. It seemed to bubble from her.

"Rumor has it that the Inn was once a brothel, of course, it was simply advertised as a boarding house after Mr. Radcliff passed away.

Stories swirl about this place. There were a lot of fights, several deaths…it all leads to ghostly tales, you know?"

I tried to interrupt, but she continued talking non-stop as we walked through the grand building, her pointing out various rooms and historically significant things as we went along. "I bought this Victorian from the great, great grand-daughter of the brothel's madam. Can you believe the same family owned it for over 100 years? Amazing. It all started with the Radcliff's. The story goes that Mr. Radcliff built this big mansion in 1895 for his wife, the love of his life. A few years later he was killed over some gambling debts, and the widow was left destitute, she had to turn the Inn into a boarding house, renting out rooms just so she could afford to keep the place. But the rooms were mostly rented to lovely young women who had a lot of male visitors. And the parties they had…" she winked at me. "It must have been one wild whore house…the things I found in this place. Wow." Her eyes were bright with excitement.

The mention of interesting historical items grabbed my attention. Antiques were one of my hobbies. Anything related to the past, to history. I loved it. "What kinds of things?" I asked inquisitively. I hated getting too many details before searching the area for ghosts but this info was too good to pass up. Plus I felt no ghosts, yet, just weirdness in the air, almost like electrical current flowing freely all around me. I could practically hear it buzzing in my ears.

"Oh, very naughty things from the brothel. All kinds of lewd and lascivious objects, very naughty objects." Her eyes glittered, and her grin was mischievous. My opinion was changing about her. At first I took her for an uptight Inn owner, suddenly I was getting a new vibe. One I thought I was going to like.

I smiled slyly, "Really? Did you keep them?"

"Of course, they have a historical connection to this place. I had to. I created a room just for all the historical 'artifacts.'" Her little air quote was emphasized with a naughty grin.

She led me to a small ladies' sitting room on the second floor that was set up a like a museum of historical kink. I gasped. There were numerous sex toys and contraptions from the Victorian era. Unbelievably bawdy pornographic photos were hanging framed on the wall and displayed all over the room- everything from daguerreotypes and tin types to more modern style images. I had never seen such a collection of antique porn. "Are these images of the women that worked here?" I asked as I walked around studying each fascinating object in the room.

"I believe most of them are. Some have names and dates on the back or along the bottom edge of the images; some had dates and names written in the cardboard frames."

"Extraordinary," I murmured as I continued to look around the room.

Corsets, bloomers, and other unmentionables were displayed in glass cases hung artfully on the wall. It was a decadent display of Victorian-era sexuality. It is quite funny that historical accounts often lead us to believe the Victorians were sexually repressed prudes. The couples and groups in the photographs were anything but prudish...and the toys were quite ingenious. In fact, many of the antiquities were quite raunchy. I loved it.

"Check out the book case." She pointed to a small bookcase in the corner. I perused the titles pulling out a few to browse the pages. Several were illustrated manuals full of sexual positions, naughty books full of hand drawn and colored nudes. It was spectacular.

"What a collection. It's marvelous."

Barbara practically radiated excitement. "I know. It sets the whole theme of this place, what I envision it to become."

I looked at her quizzically.

"I want this to be a sexual retreat. An escape where people can indulge in eroticism."

"Oh, I think I'm beginning to understand. You want me to try and get rid of the ghosts, so it has a sexy vibe, not a scary vibe."

Barbara looked away biting her lip, and I'm pretty sure she blushed, "Actually, I want you to try and get the ghosts to come out more. And indulge."

"Pardon me?" No one had ever asked me to rile up ghosts and make them more active.

"You see...the ghosts here are rumored to be...well...very randy. There have been reports over the years of guests being aroused, fondled, and pleasured by people unseen."

"And you believe this?" I asked. I had dealt with a lot of ghosts over the years- mad ghosts, confused ghosts, and mostly harmless apparitions but horny ghosts? Never, well almost never. Halloween was a different story. Ghosts tended to indulge in all kinds of fleshy decadence when the veil was lifted... and the one Halloween I spent in New Orleans...well, you can multiple that by...oh, I don't know, like a thousand. That night was the most decadently debauched ghostly encounter I had ever had- and I didn't even have sex with any of the ghosts. My vampire boyfriend whisked me away before I could be caught up in the spell.

It was the magic in New Orleans to blame for those ghostly encounters; most places didn't have the kind of mojo a ghost would need for extended fleshy interaction...even on Halloween.

"I've only been open a few months, but I've been here two years- cleaning, renovating. A lot of people have stayed with me during this time. After their stay, one couple approached me cautiously and told me about their threesome...with one of the ladies from the brothel. Later a male friend of mine woke up in the middle of the night to find himself being stroked. This continued until he was satisfied. Very satisfied. He never saw the woman, but he felt her and claimed he could smell her perfume. Another man, also alone in his room, suddenly found himself with two young and attractive women pleasuring him in ways he had only fantasized about."

"Sounds like a couple horny and lonely men with very active imaginations." I still wasn't sold on carnal haunts.

This time, Barbara definitely blushed. "I would be inclined to agree had it not been for the first account from the couple. And I have seen scantily clad women in Victorian era garb running around the house late at night. One time during renovations I walked into a bedroom and a naked couple were going at it on a bed...that wasn't there. I squeaked in surprise, and they disappeared."

"Seeing remnants of the past are one thing, but interaction, especially the sexual interaction between spirits and the living, it is crazy. I mean, if it were Halloween yes, spirits tend to crave the flesh, and when the clock strikes midnight sometimes, they get their wish. But everyday interaction," I shook my head.

"I know it sounds crazy, but I've..." she stammered, "I've not only seen the spirits but um, uh, I've had sex with them, too." Now her entire body was flushed. It crept down her neck and across her ample cleavage.

"You had sex with a ghost?" I asked incredulously.

"The first time I had just stepped out of the shower. I was applying lotion, and I felt a nudge against my bottom. I looked behind me, but nothing was there. I thought I imagined things, you know, getting easily spooked being all alone in this place. I ignored it, bent back over and continued rubbing the lotion down my legs."

She stopped and squirmed a little. "After I applied lotion to my backside, I felt a penis slide across my buttocks, nudge into my crevice and push against my opening. I freaked out and pulled away. Again nothing was behind me. Then I turned and looked into the full-length mirror beside me. A gorgeous man was behind me, his very large, very erect penis standing proud. I don't know what came over me, but I bent over and offered myself to him. As he slid into me, the room swirled and filled with mist. Voices whispered to me. I could feel caresses everywhere on my body. He continued to thrust into me. It was so...it was like nothing I ever experienced before. I came over and over. My knees were shaking, and my legs were threatening to give out when I felt him orgasm. Then, poof, he was gone." Her bottom lip was trembling, and

I could see her trying to refrain from squeezing her thighs together. Barbara was becoming very aroused just talking about the encounter.

It was getting very hot in the tiny little room filled with sexual items. I was getting very hot. I couldn't believe it, but I was being seduced by the thought of spectral sex. I stifled the urge to fan myself.

"Have you had any other encounters?" I asked. I suddenly wanted to know more. In great and explicit detail.

She giggled. "Oh yes, he's been back several times. Sometimes he brings a female friend, or two. I never imagined anything could be so erotic. The orgasms are like magic."

"And you want me to convince the ghosts to come out and play more?" I was beginning to think this job was going to be a lot of fun.

"Yes, with guests. I think the shades have become used to me, and they know I enjoy them but they are still very shy around guests, sometimes too shy and quiet. I've had several people pay a lot to stay in here in 'the haunted brothel'. They want the ghostly experience. But they are very disappointed when nothing happens."

"So people want to have sex with ghosts?" I wondered absentmindedly if there were any bad side effects from getting amorous with an apparition.

"Yes, spectrophilia is becoming quite popular. I can see why. It's amazing."

"Spectrophilia? There's a word for it?" Wow, I was behind in my ghost hunting research if I didn't even know there was a word for ghost sex.

"Oh yes, a word for it, websites about it, lots if chatroom talk, too. It's becoming the new 'thing'. I belong to the Official Association of Spectrophiliacs. There's a waiting list for the Inn once I officially open for guests. They are dying to get in here and have amazing ghost sex. If you get the chance while you are here, you should try it. I guarantee nothing could ever compare." At that point, Barbara did fan herself.

I doubt that ghost sex is that great. What I witnessed in New Orleans had been spectacular, but they weren't technically ghosts at the time. They had been fully corporeal after the veil had lifted. Anyway, I had great sex all the time. My vampire boyfriend knows how to rock my world. Woo, nothing can hold a candle to what a vampire can do when it comes to sex. My vamp is a rock solid male with centuries of skills, an exquisite sexual appetite, and has enough sex magick and pheromones to spin me into a seductive surrender in 2.2 seconds. Not that he even needed the magick and pheromones, those were just fun bonuses.

"I'll take your word for it," I said with a grin suddenly wishing Christien was with me so I could drag him to our room. I couldn't wait for him to join me.

"So, you'll take the job?" she looked hopeful.

"Sure, I'll give it a shot. It sounds a lot easier than my normal gigs. Most of the times I have to rid a place of spirits that can take elaborate research and a lot of convincing to get them to move on, sometimes even an exorcism. You just want me to let them know it's okay to come out and play."

"Yes, heavy emphasis on the coming part. Ghostly orgasms will make you see stars." The look on Barbara's face convinced me that she would be heading to her room for some boogie man banging once we were done talking.

"Great, I'm in."

"Wonderful, let me show you to your room. It's in the tower. The room has had a lot of spirit sightings but no physical contact. It was once part of Mr. and Mrs. Radcliff's adjoining suite of rooms, but later was sealed up into just one room. There is a shy doxy that haunts that room. She is petite and very busty. I catch a glimpse of her occasionally, but she never comes out to play with any of the guests. Hopefully, you can change that." With a smile, she turned and left me at the doorway to my room.

I watched as Barbara quickly and headed down the hall and enter a room at the far end by the stairs. Within several minutes, I heard some murmuring followed by moaning. My hunches were right. Barb called her ghostly boyfriend for some naughty nookie.

This was going to be an interesting job.

Chapter Two

"**Y**ou're telling me humans and ghosts are having physical intercourse?" Christien asked. He was as incredulous as I had been. "I just don't understand how. The power it would take to physically manifest is extreme, to manifest with prolonged contact. It's unheard of without a spell or power source."

"Maybe this land is a power source. I did a little research; before the Victorian Inn was built here, it was farmland. During the Civil War, a battle was fought in the area. And before that there are rumors that Native Americans lived here. That means the possibility of much bloodshed. That could power a lot of ghostly energy couldn't it?"

"Perhaps," He answered thoughtfully. "Have you seen anything yet? Encountered any tempting trollups from the other side?" His tone was playful yet I could detect a serious note underneath. Something about this haunting was not settling well with him.

"No, nothing yet," I answered.

"I'll be there tonight. Hopefully, you won't get molested by any monsters before I get there."

"Darling, the only monster I plan to be molested by is you."

"Perfect, I'll be there soon." I could hear the smile in his voice and the promise of the naughty things he wanted to do to me.

"Bring the rest of my equipment with you. I have a feeling I might need more than my 'gifts' to communicate with these sexed up spooks. For a place rumored to be so haunted and I haven't even caught a glimpse of a ghost yet ...it's weird."

"Everything is already in the truck."

"You always know what I need before I do. Do you have psychic abilities you haven't told me about?"

"No, my love, just years of experience and the ability to predict accurately, especially when it comes to you. Remember, my dear, I have been your shadow for years. I might possibly know you better than you do, considering I don't block anything or hide anything in my subconscious."

"Hmmm, you could be right. Maybe I should just consult you every morning instead of my horoscope."

He laughed, "Perhaps you should. I definitely can tell you more about your life than some crazy paragraph on a website."

"See you soon."

"Soon, my love."

After hanging up with Christien, I decided to explore. I was hoping to come across an arousing apparition or seductive spirit, but all I found was a gorgeous gardener getting off in a flower bed, his pants around his ankles. I hid behind a tree, so he didn't see me. I wanted to find out if a ghost was providing him with amorous attentions. Of course watching a tan, muscle-bound man in the throes of pleasure was no hardship for me.

It was odd, though. I didn't see anything or anyone with him but from the looks of it something was working him good. His long hard shaft jerked and thrust in the air, twitching and bobbing. His hips moved as if he thrust into someone on their knees in front of him. As I watched, several streams of semen erupted from the fat head of his cock. It hung in the air as if it landed on something I could not see. Then it was gone. Vanished.

The gardener opened his eyes. He looked baffled. He turned his head side to side looking for someone or something. Nothing was there. He quickly reached down and pulled up his pants. He walked past a gazebo, down the hill and headed to the other side of the yard before disappearing behind the house. When he was out of sight, I went over to where he'd been having his little phantasmal fuck fest. I had to see if any semen was on the ground. Just as I suspected, there was nothing. Whatever he had sex with had taken the proof with them.

Chapter Three

I continued exploring the rolling expanse of land that was all a part of the Inn's property. Most of it was wooded. At one time, it had been farmland but now only a small portion was maintained there were fruit trees and many rows of wine grapes growing up and down the hilly landscape. There was a beautiful old red barn that was well taken care of, a gazebo, and a nice size pond with a cute little picnic and beach area. The pond was kept clean so in the warmer months guests could swim in it. I glanced up at the late summer sun beating down on me, today was a great day for a swim, but I didn't bring my suit, and I was afraid the water would be too chilly for me. Michigan water is cold- even in the summer!

The brochure I found at the front desk had a map and description of the attractions on site. There was a path leading through the woods that led to an old cottage that could be rented to guests. Across the road was the old gatekeeper's cottage that now guarded a cemetery. The road had been cut through the original property, and the cemetery was now a huge public area, not just a small family plot. I wanted to explore it, though. Many of the graves went back to the 1800's and the original residents of the Victorian. Perhaps even farther back before the house was built.

I wondered if any of the girls from the brothel was buried there. If they were, I would bet they were in a different section, possibly one that was not Hallowed Ground? If the cemetery contained prostitutes from the brothel things were becoming a little clearer. Prostitutes were considered sinners and in many areas not allowed to be buried in a normal cemetery on Hallowed Ground. And if you bury a lot of people in ground that is not blessed and protected- guess what? That's right. Restless spirits.

I crossed the road and passed the stone structure that was once the gatekeeper's cottage. It now stood empty and looked un-kept. Such a shame, it was a beautiful historical stone structure that should be tended better. I continued down the path through the cemetery. It led me deep into a wooded area that seemed to circle around and lead me back toward the Inn. I came upon a clearing for a separate graveyard. It was much smaller and older than the one by the main road. There was no fence, nothing that separated it from the rest of the area. I looked up the nearby hill and could see one of the Inn's decorative steeples.

I felt the air shift as soon as I touched the cemetery ground. There might not have been a fence, but I could feel the difference. But it was not the peaceful zing of hallowed ground that sizzled in my nerve endings. No, what I felt was restless energy, radiating hunger, raw sexuality.

I tried to concentrate on the small cemetery. I needed to take in the details. Small headstones with names and dates that could barely be read adorned the lot; many only had a few legible letters left. In addition to the small stones there was a large flat rock about waist high, I looked closer. It very much resembled an altar.

Odd, why would an altar be in a cemetery? A very old but well-kept cemetery. Perhaps Barbara had been, so detail oriented that she had it restored as well. Or perhaps the family that had the Victorian all these years had tended to it and kept it from getting overgrown.

I caressed the smooth stone on the top of the altar. The energy buzzing around me grew stronger. It was erotic, enticing. Ethereal swirls pulled at my clothing, caressed my skin. Mist morphed into humanlike shapes reaching for me. I wanted them to touch me. I wanted to give myself to them. I felt hands tugging at my clothing. I crawled on top of the altar feeling the cool stone on my bare flesh.

Then a very solid set of hands gripped my arms. "LizBeth?"

I opened my eyes; it was like coming out of a trance. "Christien? You're here, already? I just spoke with you."

"LizBeth, cheri' it's been three hours since we spoke. I've been here for an hour looking for you. When I spotted the brochure, I just knew you'd come looking for this cemetery. And here you are, all caught up in sexual shenanigans with a graveyard full of ghosts."

"What? No, there were no sexual shenanigans." I protested.

"Then why are you naked?"

I looked down and gasped, my clothes were gone. Scattered all over the ground. I was completely naked. "What the hell happened?" I was beginning to get scared. The last memory I had was of hands pulling at my clothes and the cool feel of stone on my naked flesh. Did I take part in some graveyard orgy?

"The sexual energy in this place is incredible. I felt it as soon as I arrived. A kiss of vampires does not put out this much sexual energy. It's like someone dumped enough pheromones here to arouse an entire town."

"This can't just be ghosts, can it? The energy is too strong, too sexual."

He shook his head, whether it was an agreement I was not sure.

"Christien, I watched a guy get off in the garden, something was working him, but I couldn't see it. And you know I always see the spirits, even if they don't want to be seen."

"I know, cheri. Something is very off about this place, even if it is arousing as hell. I think something else is going on here. We need to do a little research on the history and background of the area. Dig deeper."

He looked me up and down, "And as much as it pains me to say this, ma cheri, you need to get dressed."

I once again looked at my clothes scattered all over the ground, "Christien, I don't know what happened."

"LizBeth, I don't think anything molested you, at least not too bad." He smirked lecherously, but I could see the worry in his eyes. "When

I arrived you were dancing, well swaying slightly. I could see things swirling around you. It was like a shadowy and sensual adult version of monkey in the middle." He laughed. "Don't worry; I don't think a little bit pleasure is going to harm you. I do not feel anything hostile here. Sexy, yes -sinister, no."

"I guess that's a good thing." I smiled weakly as I got dressed. Dancing naked I was fine with, but what happened on that altar?

"Oh yes, sexy is always a good thing." He smiled that naughty lascivious grin of his. I could see the large bulge in his trousers. This place was one big aphrodisiac.

His smile promised wicked things. And Christien's brand of wicked always meant pleasure for me. I shivered in anticipation as we headed back toward the Inn.

Chapter Four

Christien and I were alone in our room, but I couldn't get over the feeling that we were being watched. Of course, it could be the fact that the room was entirely made up of windows with nothing but see-through lace curtains.

I paced around the room wearing my flimsy nightgown. If they neighbors wanted to peer in, let them. If they watched long enough, they were sure to see something exciting. Christien and I couldn't keep our hands off each other for long.

It was warm and the air pulsed with sexual energy. I could almost hear whispers and music, the scent of perfume lingered in the air. It was hypnotic. Erotic. My body responded. I wanted...needed to feel Christien inside me

"Touch me, please," I implored. Heat and desire flooded my senses.

Christien stood up and walked over to me. Seductive and graceful with every step. He smiled that wicked and beautifully sinful grin of his. His sensuous lips curved in a way that made me want to taste them, devour them.

He took me in his arms, drawing me close and granting my wish with a kiss that scorched me, right down to my soul. His desire seared my lips, raced across my flesh and under my skin, penetrating my senses, seeking my core where it ignited liquid hot flames.

I moaned as I melted in his arms.

"This place gets you excited," he smiled.

"You get me excited," I mumbled against his lips as I kissed him again. I couldn't get enough. "Please touch me, I need you inside me."

"As the lady wishes."

His fingers found my slick center easily. Finding me ready he thrust two fingers into my swollen, achingly hot core. I undulated against his hand as I reached for him. He was so hard, so thick, so long. I yanked at his pajama bottoms needing to release his shaft so he could be inside me.

The voices continued to whisper, enticing me, suggesting such naughty things. I wanted to do them all. Feel the sensations...

I could think of nothing else. I just wanted him deep inside me. The passion rippled through me. Before my knees could give out he whisked me up and into his arms and carried me over to the wrought iron bed gently placing me on the massive king size mattress.

I sat up slightly, eying him greedily as he stood in front of me removing his pajamas.

Naked male flesh full of lean muscle rippled in front of me. Christien's cock jutted out hard and proud. I reached for him, stroking his velvet smoothness with my hand before leaning down and guiding him into my mouth.

"Ah, cheri, oui, oui, oh..." He too seemed to be under the Inn's spell as brain cells became defeated by lust. His hips rocked as he thrust his manhood into my hungry mouth. He tasted like cinnamon, exotic and comforting, sweet and spicy.

I needed to ride him. I stopped sucking on him and pulled him onto the bed with me. It took him by surprise and he tumbled down next to me. I quickly pushed him over onto his back and crawled across his beautiful hard body. I pulled off my nightgown and positioned myself above him. I found his hard shaft and guided it into me.

"You're on fire, cheri."

I rode him, moaning, crying out in pleasure with every thrust, taking him deeper and deeper into me until it was difficult to determine where one person ended and the other began. We were joined as one. But we were not alone in the room.

The air swirled around us, hot and fast until it was so thick it almost took shape. I could feel unseen hands caressing my skin, grazing my breasts, drifting across my hard nipples. The arousing sensations were soft and subtle. I could see nothing but it was undeniable that something, someone was with us.

Christien pulled me down onto his chest, "LizBeth, cheri. Hands are everywhere, touching my skin, pushing against my body. Can you see anything?" He whispered into my ear.

I tried, I opened all of my senses, used everything I had learned in my years of ghost hunting and paranormal investigations, but I saw nothing more than wispy shadows flitting about. "Barely, just shadows. But they feel so good."

"I don't understand this. Some sorcery is at play here." He mumbled into my ear as he continued to thrust his hips up to meet mine.

"Who cares, just enjoy it." I was euphoric, so drunk on desire I couldn't think straight.

Until I felt something press against my bottom. Something thick, hard and coated in slickness. Something ready to penetrate my anus. The sensation was arousing; a slight pressure opened me up, then a gentle thrust and push. The head of a ghost penis was entering my ass and it felt so amazing that it took a moment to fully register in my rational brain that something unseen was trying to sodomize me.

"Oh my God," I screamed and jumped off Christien and onto the bed, my ass buried in the fluffy softness of the mattress so nothing else could sneak up and shove itself into me.

Christien jumped off the bed ready to fight, "What is it, cheri, what is wrong?"

"Something just tried to fuck me in the ass."

He looked puzzled and looked around the room, "I think we are alone now. Are you alright?"

"I don't know...it was like I was drunk. I didn't care. I was ready to take part in a full blown orgy. Hands and caresses all over my body. It was exquisite, sensual, seductive, and sexy. It was one of the most erotic things I have ever felt. And I was good with that. Then all the sudden I realized something was trying to penetrate me. And that just felt wrong. Weird. I don't know. You know I'm no prude and it's not like you...and me...and anal..." I blushed. I didn't think there was anything Christien and I had not done sexually that was within the possibilities of what two bodies were able to do and even then we had some wiggle room with him being a vampire. He has some extra special skills humans just didn't have.

"You just didn't want something entering you that you couldn't see."

"Exactly. I mean what if it's a hideous beast or a rotting corpse or something so grotesque...if it's not horrible why didn't it show itself?"

"I do not know, LizBeth. Nothing about this place is making any sense."

"That's for sure." I sulked as I lay back on the bed looking around the room. The mood was ruined plus I wasn't sure if finishing where we left off would be a good idea anyway. It might invite the horny thing back to try to shove its invisible prick inside me once more.

Chapter Five

Christien walked into the library of the Inn looking very excited. It looked like he found more useful information than I had.

"I take it your research went better than mine?" I asked stretching my arms out behind me.

I had been sorting through the family albums, scrapbooks, and various local history books that filled the shelves while Christien went to town to do a little research. After half a day I knew minor details about pretty much the entire family that had lived here throughout the decades but none of it told me why so many spirits remained here and why they were so powerful and sexual. And invisible to me which could possibly be the strangest thing about this entire situation.

I had a feeling it all went back to the Inn being a brothel but the records from that era weren't in the library nor were they in Barbara's collection of the unique and naughty. I was exhausted and had learned nothing useful- I had not even spotted one seductive specter lurking anywhere.

The Wi-Fi didn't work so I couldn't even check online for any historical records. It had been a long day with diddley squat to show for it.

He smiled, "I think so."

He sat down beside me at the polished rosewood library table and gave me a quick kiss.

His kiss put me in a much better mood. "Well don't keep me in suspense, tell me what you discovered."

"Well after a lot of digging and a day of sweet-talking the local historian I finally got her to cave and tell me some of the darker history of this quaint little town."

"Dark history?" My interest was immediately piqued.

"Witches to be precise." He looked smug.

"Really?" I asked inquisitively. "So you think the ghosts are this powerful due to some sort of spell?"

"Hold on, cheri. Don't get ahead of the story here," he kissed me softly. The vampire knew how to shut me up. "The story Barbara told you painted widow Radcliff as an innocent woman wronged by her husband's gambling, his death left her so destitute she had to turn to a life of prostitution." He snorted, "Turns out that's not the real story. The good widow Radcliff actually drove her husband to drink. Turns out she had a way with the gentlemen of the town. And apparently she was quite wanton in her ways and didn't even bother to hide it from her husband...or anyone else. After years of being a cuckolded husband the poor man started drinking, and when he drank...he had a tendency to gamble and lose."

"So let me guess his gambling losses were piling up?"

"Yes they were. But it seems that the lovely Mrs. Radcliff had her gentlemen friends pay off his debts. Some of the holders of the debts were supposedly so 'bewitched' by Mrs. Radcliff that they even forgave Mr. Radcliff his debts. No one killed him over owed money. Mr. Radcliff killed himself. The story goes he just couldn't take the Mrs. cheating on him anymore."

"So he killed himself and she decided to make her sexuality public and become the madam of a brothel?"

"Yeah."

"So, do you think she was a witch?" The story was getting more interesting but I still was not seeing what any of this had to do with the amorous apparitions.

"I think so. I think she cast a sex spell on this Inn, hell-probably the entire town so they would be alright with a brothel in their midst."

"That still doesn't explain her behavior before the brothel or the men being so drawn to her, unless she was dabbling in sex spells for a very long time. And I don't see how that explains the randy wraiths sexin' it up around here. I mean, even if she cast a sex spell way back then, how it could it still be affecting the Inn now, so many years after her death?" The puzzle seemed to grow without the big picture getting any clearer.

"I do not know cheri but something tells me we're onto something here. There's no way Madam Radcliff and the naughty ghosts are not connected. I firmly believe there is no such thing as coincidence."

Christien sat there staring into space deep in thought. I knew he was tracing connections and going through scenarios in his head. Being around for a couple centuries had made him quite brilliant. Well, actually he had probably been brilliant to begin with, the years just added wisdom. He had proved invaluable on many of my recent paranormal investigations. He knew so much about this world that human years of working in the field could not give me. He had been living in it for centuries. He had connections and firsthand experience.

"After years of investigations I am inclined to agree, my dear. Coincidences just don't happen, not when it comes to finding answers in the paranormal world."

Chapter Six

I woke up highly aroused and bathed in the warmth of morning sunlight. One hand was on my breast, another sliding in the wetness of my sex. While a mouth suckled at the other breast. I moaned and arched my pelvis into the hand thinking Christien was waking me up for some morning love.

Then I realized it was morning, the sun was shining brightly and Christien was sound asleep next to me buried under layers of blankets and pillows. While it's a myth that vampires cannot be awake in the daytime or in the sunlight, Christien is not a morning person...er...vampire unless he absolutely has to be.

So who the hell was touching me?

I opened my eyes and sat up quickly. No one was there. The hands and mouth were no longer touching me, but I could feel a presence still in the room.

I decided to lie back down and see what happened.

I pushed the blankets aside, pulled up my nightgown and spread my legs exposing myself, welcoming the stimulating specter to give me a go.

I felt the bed shift like someone sat down, and then they moved toward me, crawling between my legs. Two fingers dipped into my wetness. I threw my head back and closed my eyes relishing in the pleasure being bestowed upon me.

I felt dreamy. Pliable. Amiable. Open to anything.

The fingers swirled in a delectable circle making me moan with pleasure as something...another finger perhaps...or maybe a thumb... gently grazed my clitoris. Amazing mini jolts of electricity spiraled throughout my body. My nipples grew taut, aching for attention. My wish was granted as a warm mouth closed over one and fingers pinched the other.

I felt a third finger join the first two inside my pussy. They began to pump in and out me, stretching and flexing a little with every thrust. The hand twisted as it moved back and forth. The relentless movement heightened my arousal making me ache for more. I wanted to be stretched and filled. And my clit needed more attention.

Again my wish was granted. Something large and phallic was pushing into my opening. It was not a penis. It felt like polished marble. When I opened my eyes I could see nothing, the sunlight was blinding. I closed my eyes and let the smoothness fill me. It was hard and cool, the girth stretching me wide, filling me like I had never been filled before. It hurt...splendidly. The mouth and fingers were gone from my breasts. They relocated between my legs where I could feel wetness and warmth pooling. It made it easier for the massive, polished dildo to move inside me. It grew warmer from my intense body heat.

Fingers exposed my aroused nub, and a warm, wet mouth closed over it. Lips sucking at it. Teasing. Then a tongue started flicking it, gently at first just a small nudge then harder and faster as the smooth marble phallus pumped in and out my pussy.

I came so hard it felt like I was convulsing on the bed. My screams awoke Christien.

He moved with lightning quickness ready to kill anything that hurt me. Once he realized my screams were from pleasure and not pain his fangs disappeared, and his eyes lost most of their glow.

He grew rock hard instantly. In a blink he was on top of me. "The scent of your arousal and satisfaction fills the room. Did you enjoy your romp with the raunchy wraith?" He nuzzled at my throat. I felt his fangs graze the tender flesh. My nether regions twitched, craving him. My body may have already had a phantasmic orgasmic experience but nothing compared to Christien when he sank fangs and cock into me at the same time.

"It fucked me with a phallic object. It was so hard, so big." I gasped.

He lowered himself between my legs, "Hmmm, your pussy is pink and swollen. Did it hurt you?"

I twisted my hips from the memory, "It hurt...so very good. I couldn't get enough. I wanted to be filled. I wanted to be stuffed full of hard marble cock."

He started licking at my heated, slick sex. My clit jumped and twitched with every flick of his tongue. My body convulsed, mini orgasms rippling through me with every lick.

"Oh god, Christien, fuck me. Sink your cock into me; sink your fangs into me. Fuck me now, I need you." I begged wantonly.

He complied without a word, sliding his thick, hard shaft into me deep and fast. Usually, he takes his time so I can adjust to his size. This time, I was more than ready, and he slid right in. All the way in. I wrapped my legs around his waist and pulled him tighter. Simultaneously opening myself for deeper penetration and creating an angle that rubbed my clit on his body.

Desire seared me like fire. I needed him to burn me out before I exploded. He was relentless as he pumped into me, rocking my body, orgasm after orgasm ripped through me, but it only made me want more.

He flipped us over so that I was riding him. And I rode him good. Hard. My head was thrown back, my long hair flowing down my back teasing and tangling his thighs. He held on to my hips tight, letting me be in control.

I couldn't get enough. The room spun with shadows. How could there be shadows in the sunlight filled room? It had been so bright.

But I could see naked figures as they appeared and disappeared, spinning in circles around me, making me dizzy. Cool hands caressed my heated flesh. Small feminine hands, large masculine hands, ghostly caresses tweaked my nipples and cupped my buttocks.

I leaned forward, putting my throat on display in front of Christien. A crazed expression drifted across his features; a wild glow blazed in his eyes. Hunger ripped through him. Fangs descended and penetrated my tender flesh. He gripped me in an intimate embrace, holding tight as he drank from me, his penis growing harder and longer inside me becoming even more engorged from my blood that flowed into him. It twitched with vampire magick sending shockwaves through me. I collapsed against him, his fangs still deep in me.

I felt large naked breasts press against my back like a woman was hugging me from behind. The breasts disappeared, and something hard, smooth and well lubricated slid against my backside. Hands spread apart my buttocks and the phallic object pushed into the opening of my anus.

"Oh god," I moaned. I couldn't fight it. I didn't want to. I let the marble phallus slide into me. This one was much smaller than the previous one. I knew it was marble from its cool smoothness as it slid easily into my over aroused body.

Gently it was eased into me, stretching my tender bits slowly until I relaxed.

It was hard to relax when I was so damn turned on and overwhelmed with sexual intensity that I thought I was going to burst completely. But I relaxed enough to enjoy the double penetration.

I was stuffed. Double stuffed. An entirely new experience for me.

Christien no longer drank from me; instead he stared wide-eyed at me. He could feel the marble shaft moving inside me, such a thin membrane separating it from his cock. I wondered how it felt rubbing against him.

He seemed to enjoy it, as he threw his head back and roared with pleasure. He thrust his hips up, slamming into my body as the woman behind me starting pumping the dildo in and out of me faster. Moving together they pistoned in and out of me, back and forth. The emotion built, the fire blazed, and the sensation was ready to boil over. Finally,

I exploded. Every nerve ending, every molecule of my body went into overdrive as the most extreme orgasm of my life ripped through me.

I screamed, moaned and thrashed as the orgasm pleasurably tore me apart. Christien held me close. I felt his body shudder, and his penis pump heat into me. It was the last sensation my body could take.

Le petit mort, my ass.

This was no little death. I collapsed. I lost consciousness.

I awoke later to Christien staring at me. His eyes were wide and full of amazement. He was also full of questions. So was I?

I sat up. The room spun, and my body tingled.

"What the fuck was that?" I felt like someone waking up the morning after a long night of drinking. Except the hangover was rather pleasant. If not a little confusing.

"Ghosts. Several of them I think." He replied.

"There was more to it than that. More than just spectral energy. Those marble phalluses...I've seen something about items like that being part of sacred sex magick. Rituals. Of course, I couldn't be sure without actually seeing them. But damn I felt them. The big one almost split me in two- and I wanted it. Craved it."

"I know. I mean I don't know, I wasn't the one getting penetrated with stone dicks, thank god, but I wanted everything that was offered. I don't think I could have said no if I tried. And to have something control me...a vampire. It must be very powerful. But it was so pleasurable, was it not cheri?" His rigid penis poked my leg.

"Seriously? I don't think I am ready for round two, Christien. Not everyone has vampire recovery. Let this human girl clean up and pull herself together before you pounce on her again, okay?"

"Sorry, my love. You know you arouse me like no other, but here...it is amplified by a hundred. I want nothing but to be buried deep inside your wetness."

Chapter Seven

"Barbara, I'm not finding what I need in the library or the brothel archives. Do you have anything about Mrs. Radcliff, perhaps any of her personal documents, a diary, anything?"

"No, I haven't found anything that was hers. Not even any photos of her. But you know, I haven't searched the attic yet. What you see around the Inn is just what I found in the rooms here. There are so many that were left untouched over the years or that just had things boxed up and put into closets and store rooms. But Tillie, the woman who sold me the Inn, she stayed in what once was Victoria Radcliff's room not the tower room she shared with her husband, but her personal room she moved into after his death. It's the biggest room in the Inn. I turned it into a suite for VIP guests. Anyway, Tillie said that she packed everything of Victoria's into trunks and had them moved to the attic. There's so much up there I just haven't got to it yet."

"Wow, with all the history you are trying to preserve, and you haven't treasure hunted in the attic?" I was shocked.

"I know, but this entire building and the grounds were stuffed with stuff. This family had a hoarding issue. In a good way, I suppose. They didn't keep crap; that's for sure, but they kept a lot. All the furniture you see here is original. All the books, albums, knickknacks, photographs, artwork, most of the linens...all of it came with the place. It took me a year just to sort, and clean things then decide what needed restoration and what could be used as is." She sighed and looked around. "I just hope all my hard work will be worth it. I hope you can get the spirits to cooperate so we can be open by Halloween."

"Maybe you should just advertise as a regular Inn. A nice Bed and Breakfast. The place is beautiful, the town quaint, and it's the perfect destination for relaxation. You have a private beach and luscious grounds, anyone looking for peace and quiet would be thrilled to stay here."

"But that's what most B&B's offer. To stand out from the crowd and succeed you need a niche. Ghosts are my niche."

"Well, I know they're here. I've felt them."

"Oh really, did you...were they...sexual feeling?" She blushed.

"Yes, my boyfriend and I had a visitor or two, twice now."

"Were you able to communicate with them?"

"If you call multiple orgasms communicating, sure, if you mean was I able to talk to them about your spectrophilia loving guests, then no. Not yet."

"Oh, well that's disappointing that you're not getting to talk to them. I am glad you experienced the mind-blowing sex, though. Wow, right?"

"You could say that." I looked around searching for the entrance to the attic. The conversation was getting way too personal. "Soooo... could I check out the attic?"

"Oh, yes of course. It's the very last door on the left; there's a staircase that will take you up. You might want to grab a few light bulbs from the hall linen closet on the right. I have no idea if any of the bulbs are burned out up there."

"Perfect. Thank you."

I wondered briefly if I should grab Christien to help me search through the attic. I decided to check it out first. If I needed him, I would come back and get him.

I grabbed a couple bulbs from the closet and opened the attic door.

It creaked horrendously like something straight out of a horror movie. Not a good sign. I flipped the switch, but no light came on. I tried finding the light fixture but couldn't see a thing. It was probably at the top of the stairs.

Feeling around in the dark I climbed the steep stairway, every single stair made a creek, squeak or awful sound of protest. It was dark, narrow and dusty, cobwebs sprawled across the stairwell. I should have brought Christien. No, I could do this. It was just an attic full of junk. In a haunted house. But I was a ghost hunter, I wasn't afraid of ghosts. There were all kinds of things that could be lurking in the dark in this weird old place.

Just then a large thud and an ungodly screech came from somewhere above me. It sounded like it was coming straight at me. I turned tail and ran down the stairs at top speed, flailing about like a madwoman, screaming the entire way down.

As I plowed through the attic doorway on the second level, Christien caught me, "Cheri, what is wrong? I was downstairs in the library and I could hear you screaming. Are you alright?"

I was panting heavily but feeling quite sheepish. What the hell was my problem? I worked with ghosts for a living...what on earth made me so scared of that attic?

"I don't know. I was overcome by fear. It sent me running down the stairs."

He looked at me oddly, then gazed thoughtfully into the stairway, "I wonder..."

"What?"

"An avoidance spell, perhaps?"

It suddenly made sense. No one had gone through things in the attic; everyone just tended to avoid it. I was overcome with fear trying to go up the stairs, which is totally unlike me. Someone had put a spell on the attic to keep people out. Which was all the more reason we had to go up there, and this time I was taking my big, bad vampire with me.

"We have got to go up there. Someone is hiding something, and we need to find out what it is."

Chapter Eight

I pushed past the fear as we slowly climbed the stairs. "Do you feel it?" I asked Christien?

"Yes, I can feel it. Though it does not stop me. Once you deny it as reality, the fear goes away."

I told myself it wasn't real, and then just like Christien said, it was gone.

I gasped when we reached the top of the stairs.

The attic was not at all what I expected. It wasn't dark or dusty at all. In fact, it was bright and spotless.

Someone was living up here. There was a large, fluffy bed surrounded by a wrought iron frame. Restraints dangled from the headboard. Whoever lived here liked to indulge in a little BDSM.

On a stand next to the bed there was a lamp...and two marble cocks. I slowly walked over to the stand and stared at the phallic objects afraid to touch them. One was massive and black. Intricately carved from black obsidian it was a perfect polished penis, though much larger than any I had ever seen in real life. I couldn't believe that monster had been inside me. No wonder I had felt so full and stretched. It was huge. The other was slightly smaller and blue, probably carved from lapis lazuli. It was as exquisitely carved and polished as the other. I could feel magick and power radiating from them. I put down the lightbulbs and picked up the large black phallus. I stroked it, remembering the way it felt stretching me.

"You were right, cheri, these are magick. Some kind of ritual sex magick is being used here. It connects everything...I just don't know how."

I put the stone cock down before I decided to shove it elsewhere, "Well whoever is controlling the magick is living here in the attic and Barbara doesn't even know. We have to find out exactly what is going on here. It may seem fun and sexy but who knows, there could be something sinister under the surface."

I knew all too well that magick and the dead didn't mix well. It rarely made for a happy ending. Even if it started as something benign, death has a tendency to distort things...

We explored the room. I found the trunks Barbara has spoken of. They were full of brothel records, receipts, and personal photo albums of Mrs. Mary Radcliff. As we continued to dig through the trunks we found more photo albums containing photos of Mary Radcliff. She was a very beautiful and curvaceous woman, which she showcased whenever possible. As we dug deeper we found that many of the photos were explicit. Extremely explicit photos. Mary Radcliff would make today's porn stars look like Catholic school girls.

The sexuality that radiated from those photographs had an odd effect on my body.

I was beyond aroused. I was intoxicated with desire. I couldn't stop looking at the photos. Mary Radcliff was erotic personified. Long dark hair, luminous pale skin, dark bedroom eyes, full sensuous lips that made you want to taste them... curves in all the right places, perfect curves. Her ass was round and ample, her breasts large and high, her body was the epitome of female perfection.

"LizBeth, look at these." Christien has opened another trunk.

I pulled myself away from the spellbinding photos. Only to find more. But these ones were in color...and looked to be very recent. But undeniably they were the same woman. Mary Radcliff.

"How?" I asked bewildered.

"I think this answers who is living here in the attic."

"Mary Radcliff? But how? This house was completed in 1895. She would be at least 150-160 years old. Could she be a vampire?"

"No, not a vampire. I would feel it, smell it. You know quite well witches can live a long time, especially if they use something to keep them young and healthy...and from the looks of it, this woman is using quite a bit of sex magick to keep things interesting around here." Christien puzzled over the situation. "But I don't see how she could keep herself so young and beautiful while feeding the ghosts enough energy to become corporeal enough to have sex with living beings."

"That would take a lot of power." I agreed halfheartedly. I felt dazed, and so aroused. I didn't really care at the moment what was going on. I just wanted to have sex. I wanted to lose myself in Mary Radcliff's beauty and watch my beloved Christien pleasure her while those carved penises were buried inside me and ghostly hands touched me everywhere.

"LizBeth, LizBeth?" Christien shook me gently, "Snap out of it, cheri. Her magick is bewitching you. We need to get out of this place."

With vampire speed and strength he picked me up and carried me down the stairs, all three flights of them and kept going right out the front door, down the hill and a couple miles down the road until we were well off the property. By this point, my head had cleared.

"Put me down, please. I am okay now."

"Are you sure, cheri? Her power had you entranced. I could smell your arousal and feel your submission. She must have been nearby."

"But what is she? She is immortal, ageless, and beautiful. Her magick is all about sex."

"And death," Christien added.

"Yes, an odd combination isn't it? Sex magick is used by witches all the time, but I've never heard of it being combined with ghosts, with sexual necromancy. This makes no sense. A witch would explain the agelessness but sex and death? How can she have such dominion over the ghosts and create such carnal energy in this house?"

"I do not know, Liz, and the fact that I don't know frightens me. And not much frightens me ma cheri."

Chapter Nine

I needed to get back into the attic. The secret to the castle spirits was hiding there. I knew it was. If I could just get over the desire that clouded my senses, I would uncover the truth.

Christien had went back into town to study land records, see if anything stood out about this area that could explain the ghostly activity and power. I was left wandering the house, restless and annoyed that I couldn't do more.

I could feel the attic calling to me. I knew it was the one place I would find answers.

So I grounded myself and attempted to cast a protective spell around me. It probably wouldn't work. Even though strong witch blood coursed through my veins, my skills at spell casting were underwhelming. Christien had been teaching me the basics about being a witch. Not an easy chore with him being a vampire. When we stayed in one place long enough his witch friends would tutor me, give me lessons in Witchcraft 101. I was a slow study. Toddlers were better at magick than I.

But I did the best I could and proceeded to the attic.

This time, I felt no fear, no intense need to retreat, in fact, the attic seemed entirely welcoming. As if it opened up and gave me a hug. And then the hug turned to a caress. My clothes disappeared as I sank onto the bed. The restraints and cuffs found their way around my wrists and ankles.

I was naked, spread eagle, and waiting anxiously for everything that was to come.

A naked woman formed out of the shadows. Intoxicatingly beautiful, dark hair, dark eyes, ruby red lips, large firm breasts...it was Mary Radcliff.

"Mary?" I asked, panting with need as she came closer. I was so wet, so eager for anything.

"Hello, my precious. You've been looking for me?" Her voice was husky, musical... a blend of sex, magick and fine wine.

"Aching for you," I responded breathily.

"Well I am here now, my sweet. Ready to pleasure you, to give you pleasure and take your desire into me."

She crawled onto the bed, crawling over me, her body grazing mine seductively. She teased me until her full breasts came to rest on top of mine. She grabbed the blue stone cock off the stand and licked it. She pushed it into her mouth, her full red lips stretching over it. I moaned, begging for it. Begging for her.

"Do you crave my beautiful stone phalluses? They are magick. They absorb the desire, the need, and the beautiful release of anyone they are used on and then power it into me, into this house, into this land. Once they were used in ancient sex rituals for fertility and prosperity, but now I use them to keep my home filled with desire."

Her breath tickled my neck as she caressed my body with the lapis lazuli phallus. She worked her way down my body, rubbing against my tender flesh. The stone cock was heated from her mouth and left a scorching trail from my neck to the opening between my legs. She stopped there and teased, trailing it around my opening, caressing my folds. She put the shaft down and used her hands to open me wide, moaning when she found my wetness inside.

"You are so beautiful, so wet, so full of desire. I will enjoy giving you pleasure and feeding on your release. Some people are only appetizers; you will be an entire four course meal." Her mouth found my clit, she kissed it sweetly before her tongue began to drive me wild. I bucked, pulling and thrashing against the restraints but I couldn't get away. Not that I wanted to.

Her tongue dipped into my wetness, twirling in circles and driving me completely mad. Oh, goddess I craved more. I wanted to be stretched and penetrated. She answered my silent plea by pushing the lapis shaft into me, the smoothness stretched and filled me. But I wanted more. I moaned and she responded by pulling out the lapis shaft and filling me with the thick black stone cock. I cried out with an intense orgasm as it slid inside me. But she wouldn't stop thrusting. I could feel my orgasms being pulled from me, being sucked into the unrelenting pleasure onslaught of the stone phalluses.

I wanted more; I wanted more sex. I wanted all the sexual things that were possible. Mary seemed to read my mind as she turned her body into a sixty-nine position and placed her beautiful pussy in my face. I greedily licked her wetness, tasting her need. I wished my hands were free; I wanted to touch her, be inside her.

Again, the woman must have read my mind because my restraints disappeared.

She answered my thoughts, "In this place, you are awarded with that you crave. Whatever you sexually desire, it will become your reality. That is the gift of my magick. My magick gives as much as it receives. It is a circle of pleasure, of give and take. Please take all that I can give. I want you to experience great joy, LizBeth. You are so very special. Let the pleasure awaken your own power."

My need was so great, I spread her wide and dipped my finger inside her. I wanted to do more. I pushed her over so that she was lying down, and I buried my face into her pussy; I pushed two, then three fingers deep into her. She moaned and thrashed under me as I sucked her clit gently while fingering her heated hole.

I wished Christien was here to share this amazing experience. And of course, suddenly he was.

"Ma Cheri, what have you gotten yourself into?" I heard him exclaim.

I looked up with a come-hither smile, "I found Mary. Please join us."

His clothes were ripped off with vampire speed and suddenly he was behind me sliding his rigid cock into my wet pussy. All of my desires were being fulfilled. All of my wishes were being granted.

As my darling vampire fucked me from behind I went back to licking Mary's delicious cunt. She tasted of honey and raspberries, so sweet and delectable. I couldn't get enough. I licked and sucked, fingered and fucked.

Then I grabbed the massive black shaft and penetrated her with it. The room filled with lightning as she threw back her head and screamed with release. Ghosts filled the room. It became a spectral orgy. The intensity pulsed through my body, making me crave such delightful sins.

I put my mouth back over her quivering flesh and sucked at her clit as she cried out once more. Her body quivered and rocked; she trembled with orgasm after orgasm. The ghosts surrounded her, covered her. Hands, mouths, all working to pleasure their mistress, to pleasure their Priestess but I suddenly knew what she needed most was a real live cock -a flesh and blood penis to complete the ritual and pump power back into her, into the house.

I sat up and moved away from her body and pulled Christien's cock from inside me. "Fuck her," I said to Christien.

Shock rippled through him. I felt his doubt. I felt his pain, he had no desire to cheat on me. "It's not cheating. I want you to fuck her, she needs a flesh and blood penis to complete the ritual. I know this, I feel it. And I crave the sight of you inside her."

"Cheri, are you sure?" He asked quietly, his cock rigid and ready bouncing with anticipation. My pussy clenched with each bounce. I needed his shaft inside her as much as she did.

"Yes, please do her for me."

He kissed me passionately then moved between her legs while I watched. I grabbed the black stone phallus. Mary's legs spread wide to accommodate him. She smiled and moaned as his long, thick cock slid into her. He spread her wide, and she took every single inch. I took every single inch of the black phallus, impaling myself upon the thick shaft. When Christien's cock was fully buried inside Mary, and the black shaft had disappeared deep inside me we all came together with the ghosts swirling around us. A complete orgy of sex and magick culminated into an explosion of orgasm and lightning. The power boomed throughout the room as sparks and bolts of lightning filled the darkness.

Then everything went black.

Chapter Ten

I awoke to a small, delicate hand stroking my face.

I opened my eyes and found Mary staring at me.

"Hello, beautiful. Welcome back to consciousness." She was still exquisitely beautiful, and still very naked. "Thank you for knowing exactly what I needed. That feeding will keep the spirits, and I powered for years."

I sat up, "I don't understand."

Christien, still naked, sat in a wooden chair by the bed. "I've figured it out. She is a succubus and a witch."

Mary smiled, "Yes that is a simplified explanation."

"Well, then. Won't you please fill in the blanks for us," he replied with his patented sexy smile.

She stood up and sauntered around the room, completely comfortable with her nudity and seemingly oblivious to the effect it had on Christien and I. His shaft was already becoming hard again and I could feel the tendrils of desire snaking out through my insides.

"My father was an incubus, sex his specialty. My mother was a witch, a Priestess, who specialized in sex magick, fertility rituals. Her family practiced their magick on this land for years; you found our altar out in the cemetery. That altar has been there for centuries. Long before the white man came here and decided that they should own everything. Something you probably don't know is that those white men your history books tell you about were not the first Europeans here, they are just the ones who wanted to take it all for themselves and claim it. My family came here over a century before Christopher Columbus sailed. My mother arrived here on a ship with my father. At the time, he belonged to The Knights Templar." She paused and turned to look at me.

I was wide eyed, astounded by the lesson in history I was receiving.

"An incubus in the Knights, the story gets stranger by the moment doesn't it?" She asked with a sad laugh before continuing her tale, "The Knights were an order of oddities. They had so many secrets, so much diversity, so much magick. Many of their members were not human. It was a safe place for wizards and other magick practitioners, until the burning times. The Inquisition forced the Knights who were not fully human into hiding, or to leave for faraway lands. My father's group ended up here."

Mary continued to strut around the room as if she were fully clothed and giving a college lecture, not naked and in the middle of a sexscapade.

"Sex and death magick often go hand in hand. My father's magick was pure sex, but his warrior side was no stranger to death. Necromancy is strong family power trait that would pop up from time to time in my mother's lineage. My mother possessed this power over the dead, but she was a good woman and preferred to focus on life and fertility. She and my father were a perfect blend of sex and death. I am the result of their love- the ultimate magickal alliance of sex and death. I can use both, bend them to my will and feed fully on either. The living give me sexual energy while the dead touch my soul... while I hold onto theirs."

She stopped pacing and knelt between Christien's legs and looked back at me with such serious eyes, haunted eyes. But then she blinked away the pain and gave me a sultry grin as she started stroking his hard shaft.

She continued her story while caressing his cock, "My mother was chased off this land by witch hunters. My father was long gone by that point. He went off to fight a war and never returned. I have no idea what happened. Incubi are hard to kill but it is not impossible. My mother brought me here as a child, some Native Americans lived on the land at the time and they took us in, gave us shelter before we had to move on to escape the witch hunters. Years later I came back and the Indians were gone. I decided to reclaim what was mine. I found a husband who purchased the land, cemetery, Native burial ground and all. Years of sex and death filled the ground. My mother had used the land for fertility rights, the natives made it a sacred burial ground then the white man started burying their dead here. Blood, sex, magick and death- this land is filled with it. And I use it, to stay young, to stay vibrant. I have the power over sexuality from both parents, the need to feed off it from my father and the need to give it from my mother. Her power also lets me control the souls that die here, even the ones that are buried here. I give them everlasting pleasure in this world."

Mary began sucking Christien's cock. His sharp intake of breath and facial contortions let me know how exquisite it was. My body ached with need as she worked her mouth on my man. I should have been angry, I should have been jealous, but I have never been like other women. Enjoying the image of my man's shaft inside another woman suddenly proved to me how different I am.

I reached between my legs and caressed my swollen flesh. It still ached from being penetrated by the phalluses and Christien, all of which are very large objects to be filled with. I moistened my clit with my wetness and began rubbing furiously. Mary stopped sucking Christien and stood up. She spread her legs over him and sank onto his cock. Slowly, seductively she slid down onto him. She stared at me while I stared at his cock sliding into her. I came when his shaft fully disappeared into her. She smiled and locked eyes with me as she rode him fast and hard. Her scream of pleasure filled the room. Once she stopped shaking from after orgasm shocks she stood up.

"Come here," she commanded me. I couldn't help myself. I followed her orders. "Taste me on his cock." I sank to my knees and licked her juices from his wet shaft. I licked and sucked eagerly, the mingling of their flavors an intoxicating delight. "Make him come," she demanded. I sucked hard, up and down, deep throating him until he bucked and shot hot semen down my throat. I sucked down every last drop.

"That's a good girl," she said as she stroked my hair. "The two of you hold such amazing sexual energy. I'm sorry, I just can't get enough of you. I don't need more, but I want it. I want it so bad. The power that the two of you create together is like nothing I have ever tasted before. Please forgive my overindulgence."

I smiled, stood up, and then sat back down on the bed. My knees were weak. "Nothing to apologize for. I think we are enjoying this just as much as you are."

Christien smiled, "Oui, very much so. Though my sweets, you have both drained me so much I am in need of other pleasurable sustenance."

"My darling, feed from me." I went to him and sat on his lap, he didn't even hesitate before sinking his fangs into me. I could feel Mary at my back, her arms went around me, hugging me as he fed from me. Her hands caressed me. I could feel arousal starting again.

I had to put a stop to this.

"Enough," I pulled from Christien and stood up. "If we keep going we'll just be having sex forever, and nothing will ever be accomplished."

Mary smiled, "What is wrong with that? We all have eternity."

"I need to finish this job and report to Barbara."

Mary looked alarmed, "Please, no. Don't tell her about me, about this. I have been able to stay so long without worry because I am cloaked. No one knows about the power, the feeding."

"I have a feeling Barbara is going to be more than willing to work with you and your needs. She wants this Inn to be a sexual retreat, one for those who have unique tastes. Like spectrophilia."

"You mean she likes the ghost sex, and her customers will as well?" Mary looked amazed. "Well, times certainly have changed, haven't they?"

"Oh, yes. For some, especially when to comes to sex. People love to indulge and experiment. You and your spirits will be well fed here, Mary. You have no worries."

She smiled, "Oh thank the, Goddess! All those years, when no one but my great-great granddaughter lived her. And none of my powers were passed to her. She had the desire of a dead fish. No sex, nothing for decades except when young family members came to visit. I was so relieved when Barbara bought the place, she's full of sexual energy. And now to hear she wants this to once again be a house of sin and pleasure." Mary kissed me passionately, "Thank you Lizbeth, I knew you were special from the moment I laid eyes upon you. You have freed me to be me again. To be a Priestess once again." She bounced up and down like an excited school girl. Except she was naked and built like a sex goddess. Her large breasts bounced erotically, I could barely tear my eyes away. I had no idea I was so fully and completely bi-sexual. I wondered briefly if these desires would remain once I left this house and Mary's presence.

"Well, we need to work things out with Barbara first but I have a feeling she will be more than willing to accommodate any needs you may have." I winked at Mary and she smiled back.

I glanced at Christien. He lounged in the chair still very much enjoying the sight of two naked women in front of him. One look at his hard shaft made me want to climb on top of him but I had to focus on completing this case so we could go home. Otherwise we'd be locked in an everlasting orgy with Mary and her spirits.

Chapter Eleven

Once we were all dressed and presentable we went downstairs to find Barbara.

I wasn't sure how she was going to handle finding out an immortal succubus/witch lived in the attic of her home and was controlling all the ghosts. Sure Barbara was pretty open minded about ghosts but succubi and witches are a whole different story.

We brought some of Mary's personal photo albums downstairs with us to prove to Mary's identity.

As luck would have it, Barbara was in the naughty room hanging several photos and shadow boxes full of more Victorian era sexual aides. She turned when she heard us walked in.

She gasped and dropped the hammer, "Mary Radcliff."

Mary looked surprised but quickly hid it behind a seductive smile. She sauntered over to Barbara, "Pleased to finally meet you, Barbara my dear." She grabbed Barbara's hand like a gentleman and kissed her delicately across the top.

Barbara looked like she would swoon at any moment, Christien moved to her side. I guess to catch her in case she did faint.

"How do you know she is Mary Radcliff? I thought you had not found any photos of her," He asked.

Barbara picked up the framed photo on the table next to her and handed it to Christien. He looked at it then handed it to me. It was Mary, in her full succubus glory. She was naked and seductively sprawled out on what looked to be the same elegant old sofa sitting in this very room. A nude man knelt between her legs while naked young women surrounded them.

I handed the photo to Mary. "Wherever did you find this?" she asked with a purr in her voice, "I thought I was careful to box up any photos of myself and take them upstairs."

"I found it last night, in a closet sticking out of a loose floorboard. Either it fell into the crack and almost disappeared under the floor or someone stuck it there on purpose trying to hide it. Your name was written on the back along with the date. August 1899." Barbara looked star-struck as she stared at Mary. You would think she had just met her favorite celebrity.

"But why assume I am Mary and not just a descendent that looks very much like her?" Mary still held Barbara's hand, caressing it seductively with her fingertips.

"Your energy, it screams sex. I could feel it as soon as you entered the room. What are you? Obviously not human, but you are no ghost either. The ghosts are all filmy apparitions, even during sex they are not wholly corporeal. But you are solid and in the flesh. Very voluptuous flesh." Barbara sighed as she looked Mary up and down.

Perhaps we should have skipped getting dressed. Barbara looked as though she was ready to tear Mary's clothes off and do her right in front of us. I had no idea she went both ways. Of course I had no idea I went both ways either until Mary enticed me.

Mary answered, "To keep it simple I am a succubus and a witch. I feed off sexual energy and the ghosts help me gather that energy."

"But you must also control and power the ghosts?"

Barbara was a lot smarter about this supernatural stuff than I expected. I should have known though, someone who is proud to proclaim themselves as a spectrophiliac surely dabbles in other supernatural studies.

Mary smiled, "I do. It is a symbiotic relationship. They feed me, I feed them, the power goes round and round and we all survive happily here in this house and on the surrounding land. As long as we have humans to feed from."

Now it was Barbara's turn to smile, "So you have no problem with me turning this castle into a Bed and Breakfast for ghost loving guests."

"Not one bit, you'll be providing the spirits and I with a smorgasbord of energy. But just to be clear, you are fine with the fact that I live here, have always lived here, and that I am not human?" Mary asked Barbara inquisitively. It was probably hard for her to adjust to humans being so open about "Others". She came from a time when they killed witches or anyone that was different.

"Of course, it's so wonderful. I have so many questions...I am such a history nerd...this is going to be amazing having someone to ask that actually lived through the Victorian era. Plus you and the ghosts are going to make this the destination for spectrophiliacs everywhere- and for all those curious about spooky sex and amorous apparitions." She laughed a joyous sound that made me smile.

"Wonderful, I will make sure the spirits now know they are more than welcome to come and play with the visitors."

I had a question for Mary, "Why haven't I been able to see the ghosts? With my powers I always see them, even when they don't expect me to."

"Sorry, my dear. That was my fault. I had the entire castle and surrounding area under a spell so nosy ghost seekers wouldn't see the spirits and try to banish them. The last thing I need is an exorcism ripping my ghosts away. I can fight the ritual, but it takes so much energy. I wanted to avoid that. For years I have been running on fumes with that old lady being the only full time resident."

"How have you fed with no one sexually active living here?"

"I am not stuck here, so I can leave and feed. Or bring people back here to feed on, but it made us all weak not having constant energy flowing into the land and the house. I had to power all of us on just what I could acquire elsewhere. If I could lure someone back here that helped, the ghosts and I could all feed. The ghosts would also go out occasionally to the cemetery and seduce the caretakers, groundskeepers and visitors. But the sexually energy of those visiting a cemetery is not hot and full of desire."

Suddenly Barbara hugged Mary, "You don't have to worry about that anymore. I already have a waiting list of people who want to stay here- and they are all full of desire."

"I can't wait," Mary replied with a hungry grin.

"Can you and the ghosts help me get this place ready to open? The sooner it happens the sooner you will have a continuous source of sexual energy."

Mary's eyes lit up, "I can put everything to play so this Castle will be ready for guests within two weeks."

"Really?"

"Really."

Barbara squealed and jumped up and down with delight. We all laughed at her enthusiasm.

Chapter Twelve

True to Mary's word the Castle Inn was open for guests within two weeks. Just in time for autumn festivities. People are always more interested in ghosts and haunted houses around Halloween. The Castle was always packed to the limit, even the guest house outside the castle was rented out every night.

Christien and I checked in every couple weeks to make sure that things were running smoothly.

In mid-October Mary invited us to a Halloween Masquerade Ball.

"Liz, it's going to be so grand. It will be the first time I get to use the ballroom for what it was truly meant for. Please tell me you and Christien will come. It will truly be a Ghostly Gala- dress to impress, masks required."

How could I say no? The last Halloween Ball I attended had been in New Orleans. It was time to dust off my mask and pull my ball gown out of storage.

"We wouldn't miss it, Barbara."

"Awesome, I'll save you a room. I can't wait to see you again. See you on Halloween Eve, the party is October 30 and will go into Halloween. Oh when that big Grandfather clock strikes midnight...LizBeth...I am so excited."

"Oh, Barbara. I'm excited too. We'll be there."

I hung up and told Christien about the Halloween party.

"That should be interesting," He said with a hint of sarcasm.

"What do you mean? It will be fun."

"Do you remember the power of the ghosts in New Orleans on Halloween? The ghosts at the Castle Inn are stronger. I imagine in a night when they can take on flesh…it is going to be one wild event."

"Oh…I didn't even think of that. Well now we definitely can't miss it." I laughed.

"You just wish to see Mary again," he sniffed as if hurt.

I knew he was just joking. I knew he would be happy to see her again too. The thought of the three of us together again… "I do wish to see Mary, I'd also like to see Barbara. Plus you know I love Halloween. We haven't dressed up for Halloween since we left New Orleans. It's time we dusted off our masks."

He leaned over and kissed me, "Ma cheri, whatever you wish. It is yours."

Chapter Thirteen

The Castle was ablaze with light, the epitome of Victorian Halloween Elegance, with a modern twist. The entire castle looked as if lit up with candles and gas lamps...but it was all electric lighting made to look like flickering flames. I loved it. The melding of old and new blended seamlessly.

Christien drove us up the long twisting driveway and stopped at the Valet gate. Fancy. Barbara had gone all out. I was giddy with excitement.

A fancy man in tuxedo tails and an elegant mask opened my door and helped me from the car. He presented me to Christien and bowed as he backed away. I felt like royalty.

The path was lit with pumpkins and lanterns and the wraparound porch was filled with Victorian styled Halloween elegance. The bistro tables all held centerpieces of skulls and ravens, very Edgar Allen Poe. Costumed party goers milled about drinking, laughing and smoking on the porch. Each costume more beautiful than the last, my eyes senses were in happy overload and we had not even entered the Castle yet.

As we reached the entrance another man in a tuxedo opened the door for us. My eyes tried to take in everything at once as I walked in. The entrance was filled with fog and the flickering of candlelight. Spooky music played softly. A sign pointed to the dining area for refreshments and to the ballroom for dancing. Another sign listed where the fortune teller could be found and where and when the séance would be held.

Victorian Halloween fun at its best, no Victorian Halloween event was complete without a fortune teller and medium.

Sparkling spiderwebs and glittering gauze accented the décor. The chandeliers sported assorted Halloween finery and the normal art and photos that filled the walls had been replaced with darkly beautiful images and Victorian inspired silhouettes.

"It's beautiful, Christien, what do you think? Is it authentically Victorian?"

He looked around, "As close as you can get in this modern age. I think Barbara took some of the best ideas and designs and improved on them. I approve," he smiled and brought my hand to his lips. His lips gently brushed my flesh, sending ripples of excitement through me. Eleven years together and he still made my heart race and my blood turn to liquid fire. "Anything that makes you happy gets the stamp of approval from me."

"So glad to hear that," Barbara quipped as she met us at the entrance to the ballroom. "I am thrilled that you guys love it. I've worked so hard, and I think it's a success. We sold out of tickets and the Castle is completely booked. I hope you guys don't mind, I ended up putting you in the guest house out back. Everyone wanted to be in the main house for the hauntings."

"Barbara, my lady, you look absolutely stunning tonight. And please do not fret. I'm sure we'll enjoy the guest house quite a bit." Christien winked at her, and charming as always took Barbara's hand and brushed it with his lips. I watched her shiver in delight.

She blushed and giggled and she ushered us into the ballroom. He was right, she did looking stunning. Actual I think breathtaking was a better description. Her blond hair was swept into a gorgeous updo with romantic tendrils of curls framing her face and drawing attention to her long slim neck. A cameo pendant hung amidst her ample cleavage, made more ample than usual by the corset she wore. Her gown glimmered with blue black shine, a metallic fabric that changed color with the light and made her blue eyes shimmer with mischievousness. Trimmed with black lace that matched her black lace mask, she was the picture of Gothic Halloween perfection.

"Barbara, it's so good to see you again. You look breathtaking tonight. Exquisitely beautiful."

She beamed with delight at my words, "Thank you Liz. I'm so excited. This party is the culmination of all I've worked so hard for. I really do hope you enjoy yourselves tonight. Please join the party and enjoy. Dancing has begun, food will be on the buffet soon. Right now we just have drinks and appetizers in the dining room. At 7pm an Edgar Allen Poe look alike will be doing a reading of The Raven, The Telltale Heart and Annabel Lee in the library. The haunted tour starts at 8pm, not that you guys need that. You had a back stage pass before we even opened. The séance is at 9pm, and the fortune teller will be taking clients all evening-every twenty minutes. LizBeth, I hired the medium and fortune teller from recommendations made by your assistant Carrie. I wanted the real deal, not charlatans."

"Then I am sure they are perfect. Carrie's database of Others working professionally for humans is very exclusive. She would not recommend anyone she had not personally vetted." Carrie had a side business that I supported whole heartedly. She referred Others for professional services humans needed- ghost hunting like myself, as well as those who worked as psychics, mediums, fortune tellers, healers, exorcists, banishers, spell casters and the like. She also connected vampires, succubi and incubi to willing donors. It made things much easier than hunting for prey and hoping no one got hurt. This service made sure everyone got what they needed and was satisfied at the end. It was quite brilliant.

My desire was getting the best of me, I couldn't wait another moment, "So where's Mary?"

Barbara laughed, "Oh you know her, she's being the belle of the ball and enjoying the spotlight. I'm sure she's fed her hunger enough already to last for months. The lust in the air tonight is so thick even I can feel it. And between her and ghostly girls...they are fanning the flames of desire into a whirlwind that will surely become a storm of carnal decadence before the night is over. At least that's what I am hoping for. That's why everyone has paid good money to be here tonight."

"The Castle is already alive with sexual activity," Christien murmured. "I can hear the moans of pleasure and smells the scent of sex."

"Oh yes, dark corners are filled with naughty couples making out. Several rooms already have small orgies taking place with a combination of party goers and sexy specters, and I spotted one couple in the hallway partaking in a very public display of oral affection." Barbara laughed. "I have been groped by so many hands tonight I've lost count. But I am not complaining. I love every second of it."

"As long as everything is consensual and everyone is happy then there is nothing at all to worry about." I replied. I was more than ready to partake in a little groping myself, hopefully with Mary. I glanced at Christien, he was staring longingly into the ballroom. I wondered if he spotted Mary or was just aching to join the fun.

I stood on my tippy toes to whisper in his ear, "See something you like?" I purred.

He turned to me and smiled, "Oui, ma cherie."

"Then by all means, let's join the fun."

"After you, my lady," he bowed towards the open doorway.

I turned to Barbara and gave her a hug and a kiss on the cheek, "Make sure you take time to enjoy yourself tonight, you've earned it."

Her eyes twinkled as she hugged me hard, pressing our breasts together. She kissed me on the lips and gently pushed her tongue into my mouth. I hungrily kissed her back. She pulled away with a naughty grin, "Sorry, I've wanted to do that since the moment we met."

Breathlessly I replied, "No apologies necessary. I quite enjoyed it."

"Good," she winked at me, "I hope that heightens your appetite for tonight."

Oh yeah, my appetite was in overdrive. I was ravenous.

I grabbed Christien's hand, "Come on darling, it's time to get our freak on."

He laughed as we entered the ballroom.

I spotted Mary on the other side of the room and became giddy with excitement.

I had a feeling this was going to be better than Halloween in New Orleans.

About the Author

ROXANNE RHOADS is an author, book publicist, mixed media crafter, and lover of all things spooky. Her non-fiction books include *Haunted Flint* and *Pumpkins and Party Themes: 50 DIY Designs to Bring Your Halloween Extravaganza to Life*. She is the owner of Bewitching Book Tours, a virtual book tour and social media marketing company and she operates a Halloween blog- A Bewitching Guide to Halloween. She sells handcrafted jewelry, art, and home decor through her Etsy store The Bewitching Cauldron. When not reading or writing, Roxanne loves to craft, plan Halloween adventures, and search for unique vintage finds.

https://www.patreon.com/RoxanneRhoads
https://www.tiktok.com/@roxannerhoads76
https://www.abewitchingguidetohalloween.com/
https://www.bewitchingbooktours.com/
https://twitter.com/RoxanneRhoads
https://www.instagram.com/roxannerhoads/
https://www.facebook.com/ABewitchingGuidetoHalloween/

Don't miss out!

Visit the website below and you can sign up to receive emails whenever Roxanne Rhoads publishes a new book. There's no charge and no obligation.

https://books2read.com/r/B-A-PFIB-BXAI

BOOKS 2 READ

Connecting independent readers to independent writers.